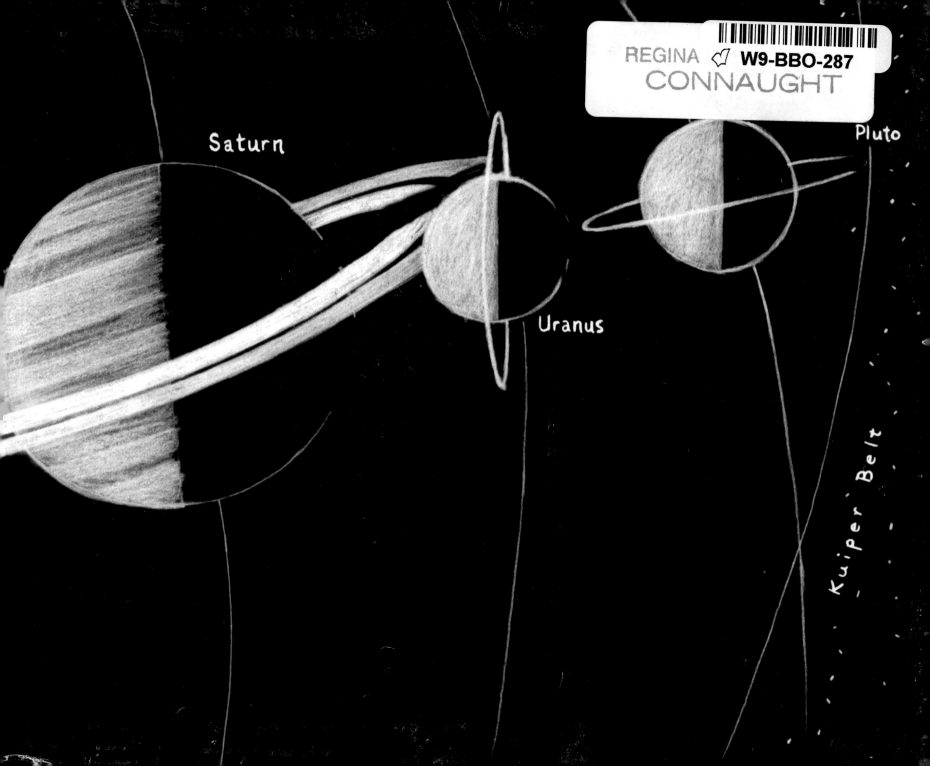

REGINA
CONNAUGHT

W9-BBO-287

TOUCHDOWN MARS!

An ABC Adventure

Peggy Wethered and Ken Edgett illustrated by Michael Chesworth

G. P. PUTNAM'S SONS   NEW YORK

For Elisabeth and Melissa
—P.W.

For Adam
—K.E.

For Mrs. Damon, my first-grade teacher
—M.C.

Thanks to Ken and Peggy for sharing your up-to-date knowledge of Mars and exhaustive energy for fact-checking,
thanks to Refna Wilkin and Susan Kochan. And my special thanks to Cecilia Yung. —M.C.

Text copyright © 2000 by Peggy Wethered and Ken Edgett. Illustrations copyright © 2000 by Michael Chesworth.
All rights reserved. This book, or parts thereof, may not be reproduced in any form without permission in writing from the publisher.
G. P. Putnam's Sons, a division of Peguin Putnam Books for Young Readers, 345 Hudson Street, New York, NY 10014.
G. P. Putnam's Sons, Reg. U. S. Pat & Tm. Off. Published simultaneously in Canada. Printed in Hong Kong by South China Printing Co. (1988) Ltd.
Book design by Marikka Tamura. Text set in Triplex Bold and Oz Handicraft.
The illustrations for this book were painted with watercolor and ink on Arches Cold Press watercolor paper.
Library of Congress Cataloging-in-Publication Data
Wethered, Peggy. Touchdown Mars! : an ABC adventure / by Peggy Wethered and Ken Edgett ; illustrated by Michael Chesworth.
p. cm. Summary: An alphabet book which presents facts about a space expedition to Mars. 1. Space flight to Mars—Juvenile literature.
2. Mars (Planet)—Exploration—Juvenile literature. 3. English language—Alphabet—Juvenile literature. [1. Space flight to Mars. 2. Mars (Planet)
3. Alphabet.] I. Edgett, Ken. II. Chesworth, Michael, ill. III. Title. TL799.M3W48 2000 919.9'2304—dc21 [E] 98-39592 CIP AC ISBN 0-399-23214-1
10 9 8 7 6 5 4 3 2 1 First Impression

You are an astronaut! These are your crewmates. You are going to Mars!

An astronaut can be a woman or a man. You must study and train very hard to prepare for travel in space. Astronauts work together as a team.

B You are ready to board your rocket!

When you board the spacecraft, you need to be sure you have enough supplies for a three-year mission. Your supplies include food, water, and clothing.

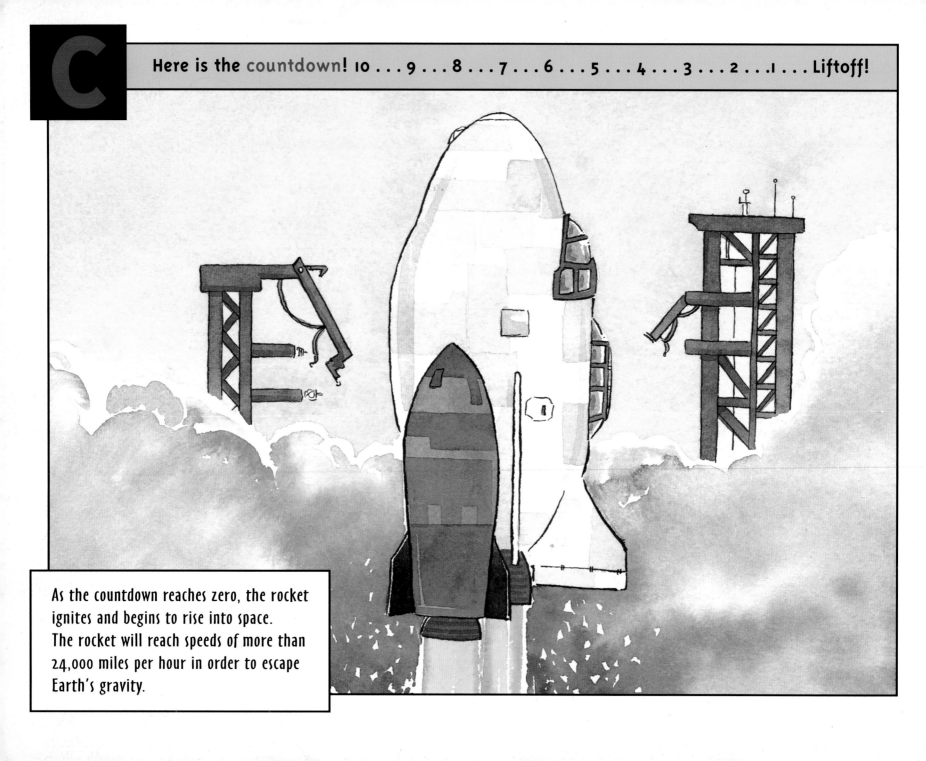

As the countdown reaches zero, the rocket ignites and begins to rise into space. The rocket will reach speeds of more than 24,000 miles per hour in order to escape Earth's gravity.

You are going up . . . up . . . up . . . in the right direction.

D

Mars, often called the "Red Planet," is fourth from the sun. Once your rocket has left Earth, the direction your spacecraft will go is farther away from the sun, out toward Mars.

Earth will look very different on your way to Mars. Imagine it appearing smaller and smaller until it looks like a blue star. Earth appears blue because it is mostly covered by oceans. The water reflects the blue color of Earth's sky.

E Look out the window. Wave good-bye to Earth.

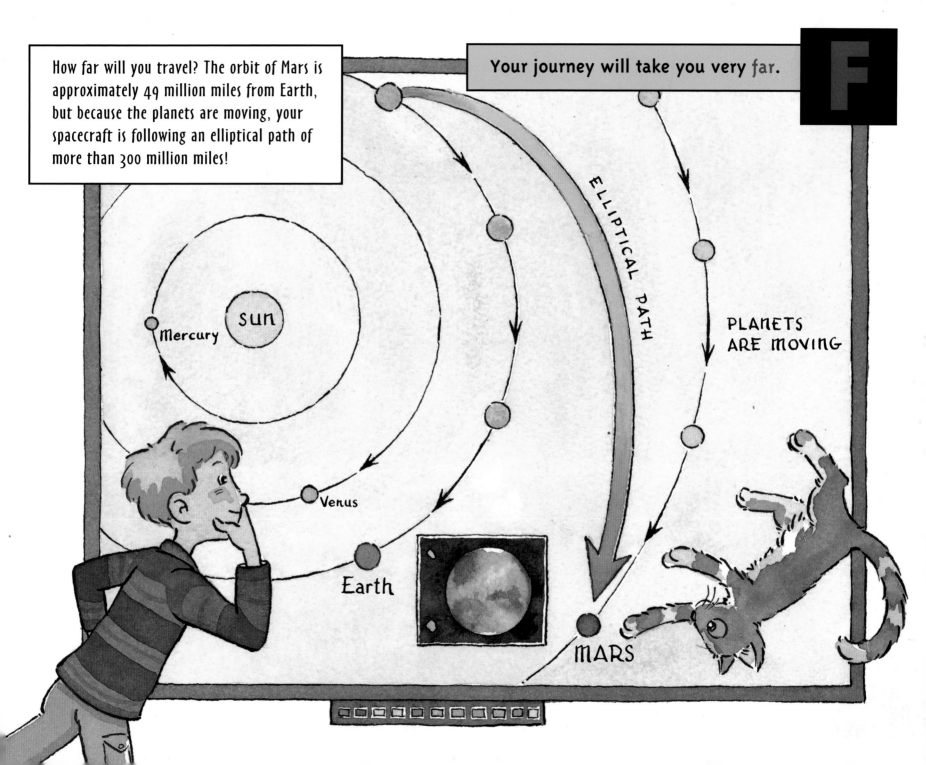

How far will you travel? The orbit of Mars is approximately 49 million miles from Earth, but because the planets are moving, your spacecraft is following an elliptical path of more than 300 million miles!

Your journey will take you very far.

F

ELLIPTICAL PATH

PLANETS ARE MOVING

sun

Mercury

Venus

Earth

MARS

In space, you do not feel the pull of gravity. Everything seems to float . . . even you!

G

Once you get to Mars, you will feel gravity again, but it will be much less than on Earth. Because the gravity is different, a person that weighs 100 lbs on Earth would only weigh 38 lbs on Mars.

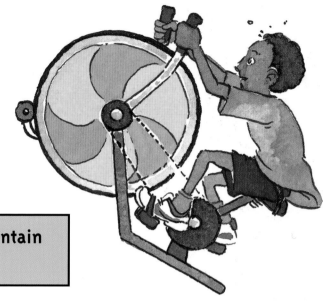

On your trip to Mars, you maintain your normal healthy habits.

Your healthy habits include daily exercise, brushing your teeth, washing your hair, and keeping your sleeping quarters clean.

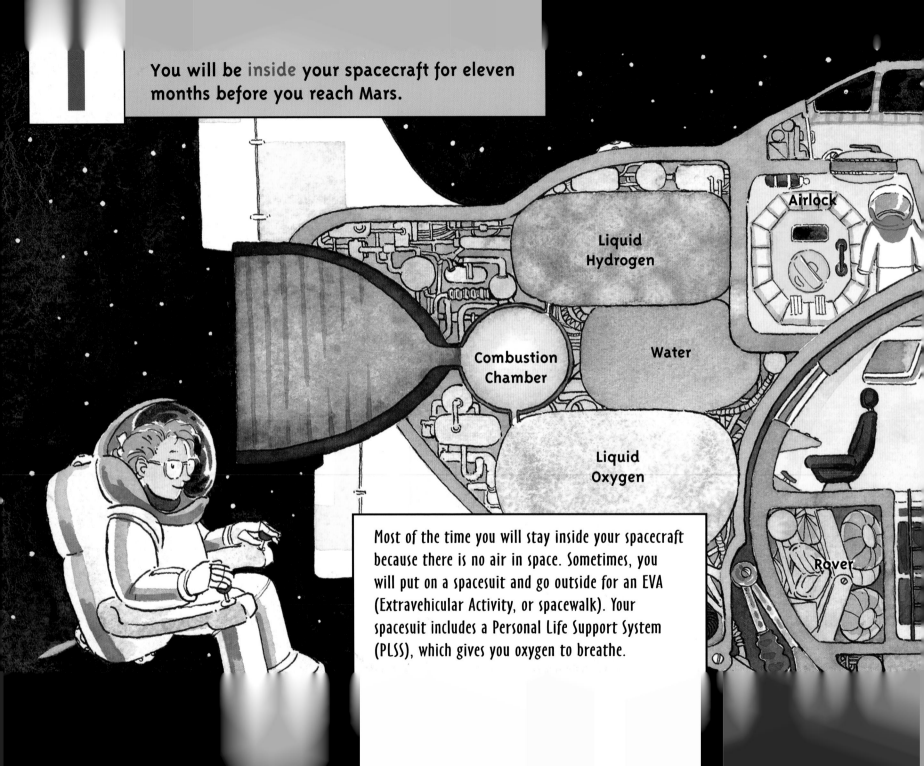

You will be inside your spacecraft for eleven months before you reach Mars.

Airlock

Liquid Hydrogen

Water

Combustion Chamber

Liquid Oxygen

Rover

Most of the time you will stay inside your spacecraft because there is no air in space. Sometimes, you will put on a spacesuit and go outside for an EVA (Extravehicular Activity, or spacewalk). Your spacesuit includes a Personal Life Support System (PLSS), which gives you oxygen to breathe.

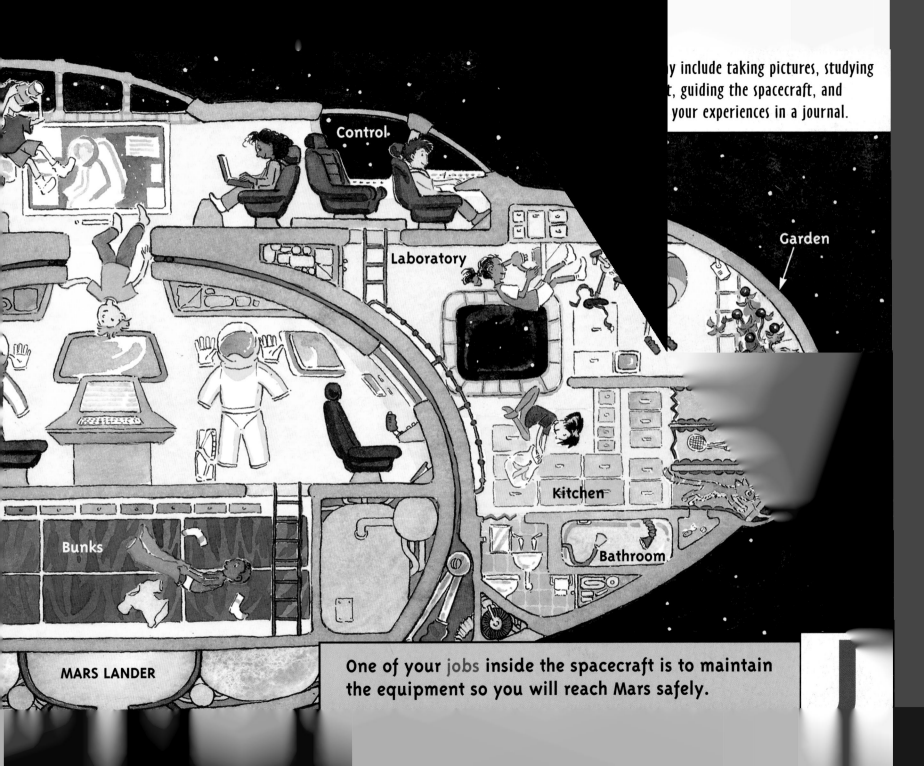

y include taking pictures, studying
t, guiding the spacecraft, and
your experiences in a journal.

Control

Laboratory

Garden

Kitchen

Bathroom

Bunks

MARS LANDER

One of your jobs inside the spacecraft is to maintain
the equipment so you will reach Mars safely.

You know you are getting closer to Mars because it is appearing larger and larger every day. Your knowledge of this planet will grow and grow after you arrive.

Your spacecraft's computers are programmed with the knowledge necessary to automatically fire small rockets at a precise moment to slow your vehicle.
This will put the spacecraft into orbit around Mars. You can't wait to get there and start exploring!

Your spacecraft will stay in orbit around the planet. You will get inside a lander, which will separate from the main spacecraft and land on the surface.

The day has finally come. Your spacecraft is in orbit, and now you are going to land on Mars!

L

M The landing craft takes you down . . . down . . . down . . . *poof*. You are on Mars!

Mars is about half the size of Earth. The surface looks red because of the iron oxide (rust) in the soil.

Each person in the crew puts on a spacesuit. Back on Earth, people of all nations are watching your adventure on television!

You are excited to be on Mars. You and your crew have come from many nations of Earth.

O You open the hatch and step outside.

Imagine what it will be like to step outside on Mars. The sky might appear light brown or pink because of the dust picked up by the wind. The ground may be soft, dry, and powdery.

You take your first steps on the planet Mars, leaving your footprints.

P

Like our own planet Earth, Mars is a world that changes over time. Look at your footprints. They might disappear next time a strong wind blows.

Q You have come with many questions. Now you begin to explore.

What questions do you have about Mars? Do you think there was ever anything living on Mars? What has made this planet look so different, yet so similar, to Earth?

The first thing you do is collect some Mars rocks to take home to Earth.

You may find that most of the rocks are similar to the ones you can find on Earth. Many of the rocks might come from lava flows and volcanoes.

R

You look around and check out the scenery. What do you see?

S

The scenery will be very different on Mars than on Earth. You may see huge canyons like the Valles Marineris. This system of canyons is much larger and more complex than the Grand Canyon on Earth. The Valles Marineris would stretch across the entire United States—a distance of nearly 3,000 miles.

Although the temperature is much colder than on Earth, you keep warm inside your spacesuit. Temperatures on Mars are usually below 0°F, but a really warm day near the equator might get up to 70°F.

You visit the martian north pole. The thermometer says the temperature is almost two hundred below zero. *Brrrrrrrrrrrrrrrrrrrrrrrr . . .*

T

TEMP: -172°F

LIVE FROM PHOBOS

U Look up in the sky. Mars has two tiny potato-shaped moons!

Up in orbit around Mars are two moons, Phobos and Deimos. Phobos ("fear") is larger than Deimos ("dread"); it is about 17 miles across. Compare that to our moon, which is about 2,000 miles in diameter.

The largest volcano in the solar system is on Mars. Olympus Mons is about 15 miles high. It is approximately 375 miles across at the base, and its caldera (the crater at the top) is nearly 50 miles across.

You explore huge valleys and giant volcanoes!

V

The weather on Mars is very predictable. Most days, the sky is clear and cool. Light breezes might blow in the early morning and late afternoon.

The weather on Mars isn't always calm. Sometimes there are vigorous dust storms. The dust storms have been known to cover the whole planet! The weather also changes with the seasons. Like Earth, Mars has winter, spring, summer, and autumn.

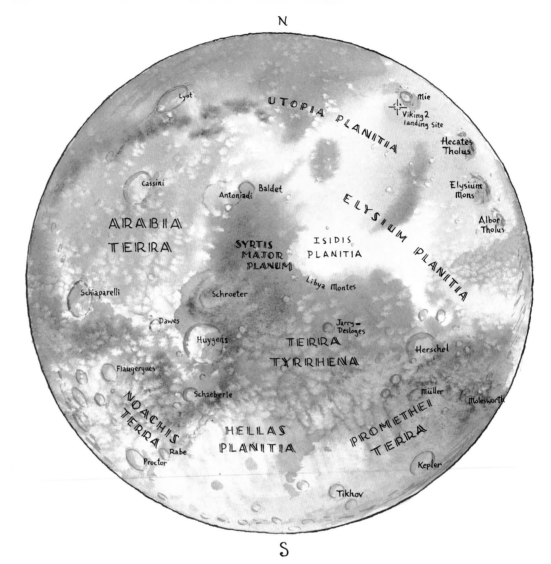

N

VASTITAS BOREALIS

Perepelkin

ARCADIA PLANITIA

Milankovic

Alba Fossae

Tantalus Fossae

ALBA PATERA

TEMPE TERRA

ACIDALIA PLANITIA

Lycus Sulci

Mareotis Fossae

Tempe Fossae

Ceraunius Fossae

Kasei Valles

CHRYSE PLANITIA

AMAZONIS PLANITIA

Olympus Mons

Ceraunius Tholus

LUNAE PLANUM

Viking 1 landing site

Ascraeus Mons

THARSIS MONTES

Tharsis Tholus

Pathfinder site

Ulysses Patera

XANTHE TERRA

Biblis Patera

Pavonis Mons

Candor Chasma

Juventae Chasma

Arsia Mons

VALLES MARINERIS

SYRIA PLANUM

Oudemans

SINAI PLANUM

Vinogradov

Memnonia Fossae

Claritas Fossae

DAEDALIA PLANUM

Holden

Bernard

Mariner

Sirenum Fossae

Ma'adim Vallis

Newton

Icaria Fossae

ICARIA PLANUM

Bosporos PLANUM

AONIA TERRA

NOACHIS TERRA

TERRA SIRENUM

Slipher

Lowell

ARGYRE PLANITIA

S

X marks the spot of your greatest discovery. What do you find there?

On this map, the "X" is in western Candor Chasma in the Valles Marineris canyon system. This area has many outcrops of layered and eroded rock. Geologists use rocks to study the history of a place. You pick at layers of bright, crumbly rock with a rock hammer. You examine fragments with a magnifying glass. What do you see?

Your time on Mars is one Earth year long (365 days). That is how long it takes before the two planets are in the right position for the trip home.

Your **year** of exploration on Mars is complete. It is time to head home. You are going back to Earth.

After leaving Mars, you first rendezvous with the larger spacecraft you left in orbit a year earlier. This craft will take you to Earth. Assuming you have zero problems, you will be back home in eleven months. Have a great trip!

You and your crewmates are ready for launch. Five, four, three, two, one . . . zero!

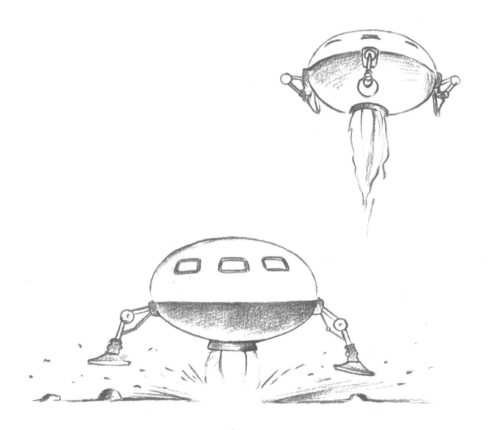

Mars A-B-Cyclopedia

A The atmosphere of Mars is made mostly of carbon dioxide (95%). The atmospheric gases also include nitrogen (3%), argon (2%), and others. Oxygen makes up less than 1% of the air.

B Basins are large, circular, low areas on Mars that were formed by the impact of very large asteroids early in the planet's history.

C Craters of all sizes cover much of the martian surface. They are caused by the impact of comets and asteroids. Such craters are common on Earth's moon and other planets and moons in our solar system. The largest craters are also called basins.

D Mars is a cold desert world with no liquid water. This dry planet has many sand dunes and wind-sculpted hills. Dust storms are common in some regions such as Noachis Terra and Hellas Planitia.

E At its equator, Mars is about 4,220 miles across, just about half the size of Earth.

F Giant faults and fissures (cracks) are found in various locations on Mars. They are caused by splitting of the martian crust. In some places, it looks like water might have come out of some of these cracks.

G Geologists have been studying the surface of Mars since the *Mariner 4* flyby in 1965. This was the first spacecraft to reach the planet. Its pictures revealed that the surface is heavily cratered.

H Hellas Planitia is the floor of one of the oldest and biggest impact basins on Mars. It has several volcanoes around its rim, and some scientists think that it was once filled with water to make a sea. "Hellas" is an old word that refers to ancient Greece on Earth.

I Mars has two ice caps. One is at the north pole, the other at the south pole. They contain a mixture of frozen water, frozen carbon dioxide (dry ice), and dust. The polar caps get bigger in winter and smaller in summer, as the seasons change.

J Juventae Chasma is one of several large canyons that appear to have been created by the splitting of the martian crust, followed by landslides and possibly the release of water in massive floods.

K Kasei Vallis is a giant flood channel carved by water. "Kasei" is the Japanese word for Mars. Many of the channels on Mars are named for "Mars" in other languages.

L Percival Lowell was an astronomer who in the 1890s and early 1900s popularized the idea that Mars was inhabited by an intelligent civilization. Today, no one expects the planet to have creatures like people or animals, but microscopic organisms such as bacteria are still considered possible.

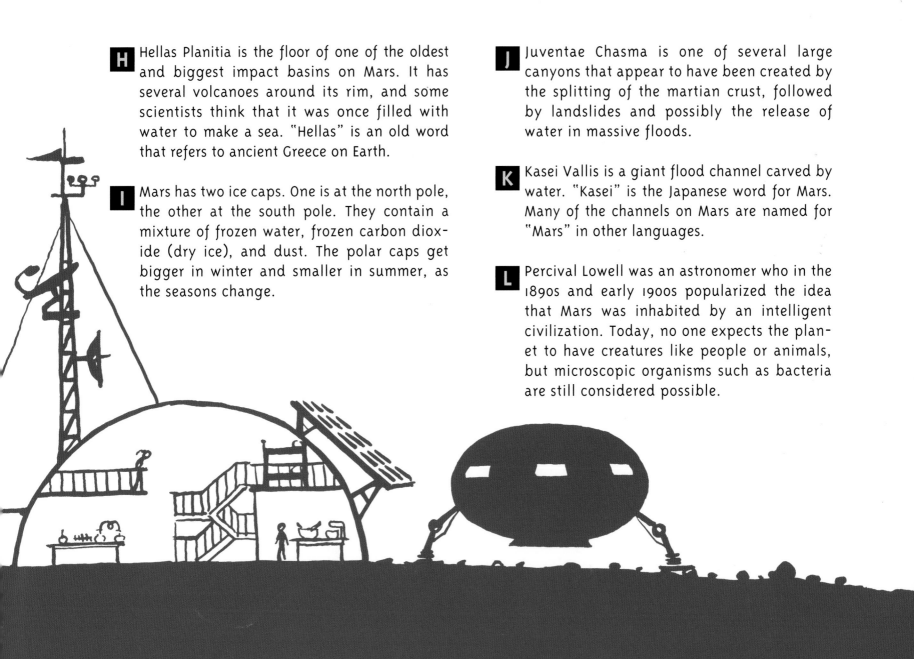

M Mountains on Mars are either high, broad, shallow-sloped volcanoes (like Olympus Mons), or they are arcuate (curved) ranges of small, sometimes steep hills that compose the rims of old eroded impact basins.

N Nirgal Vallis is a long curvy channel that might have been caused by water some time in the martian past. "Nirgal" is the ancient Babylonian word for Mars.

O The Olympus Mons volcano is more than 3 times the height of Earth's Mt. Everest, and is so wide that it would cover the entire state of Arizona in the U.S.A.!

P *Mars Pathfinder* and the small rover *Sojourner* landed on Mars on July 4, 1997. This mission lasted about 83 days, with the rover exploring nearby rocks while the lander monitored weather and examined the color of the sky and surrounding terrain.

Q Many successive Mars quakes probably caused the fissures and giant canyons on the surface. Earthquakes on our homeworld move the planet's crust and create cracks and fissures in the ground, too.

R Mars rotates on its axis every 24 hours and 37 minutes, making a Mars day slightly longer than Earth's 24-hour day.

S seasons on Mars, as on Earth, result from the tilt of the planet's axis and its orbit around the sun. The axis of Mars is tilted about 25 degrees, similar to the 23-degree tilt of Earth's axis.

T The Tharsis region on Mars contains the largest concentration of volcanoes. This area is larger than the western United States, and has huge lava flows and volcanoes like Arsia Mons, Ascraeus Mons, Pavonis Mons, and Olympus Mons.

U Utopia Planitia was visited by the *Viking 2* lander. It touched down in September 1976, and operated until April 1980. During the cold martian winter, *Viking 2* took pictures that showed frost on the surface.

V Many small branching valleys are found in the ancient cratered terrains of Mars. These appear to have been formed by water, either from run-off of rainwater or snowmelt, or—more likely—by the slow sapping and seepage of ground water.

W Liquid water does not exist on the surface of Mars today because the atmosphere is too thin (100 times thinner that Earth's). Such low atmospheric pressure causes frozen water to go directly from solid ice to water vapor with no liquid stage in between.

X Xanthe Terra is a region north of the Valles Marineris that has many craters and is cut by giant flood channels. This region, like all other parts of Mars, has a complex history that scientists are only just beginning to understand.

Y Young surfaces on Mars give geologists clues about recent events in the planet's history. The oldest areas on Mars have many craters that were formed billions of years ago, while younger surfaces have fewer craters.

Z Zuni, Zulanka, and Zir are some of the craters on Mars named for small towns and villages on Earth. Zuni is named after Zuni, New Mexico, U.S.A. Zulanka is in Russia, and Zir is in Turkey.

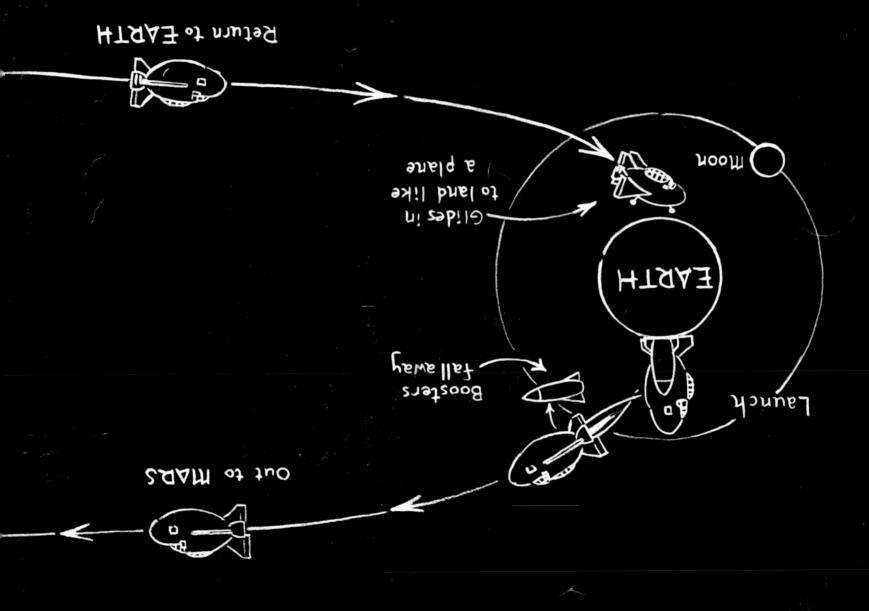